# Beyond T
( Brea

# Beyond The Pits 2

**Beyond The Pits, Volume 2**

Abdul-Hafiz Azumah Hamza

Published by Abdul-Hafiz Azumah Hamza, 2024.

This is a work of fiction. Similarities to real people, places, or events are entirely coincidental.

BEYOND THE PITS 2

**First edition. October 13, 2024.**

Copyright © 2024 Abdul-Hafiz Azumah Hamza.

ISBN: 979-8227964298

Written by Abdul-Hafiz Azumah Hamza.

## PREFACE

In the depths of human history, there exist tales of ancient civilizations, hidden villages, and mysterious lands. The stories of these places are often concealed in myth and legend, passed down through generations by word of mouth. But what if the myths were true? What if the legends held secrets to unlocking the mysteries of the universe?

In the following pages, we delve into the story of one such village, hidden away in the heart of Africa. A place where ancient magic still lasts, where the land holds secrets, and where the past and present collide. This is a tale of courage, sacrifice, and the unbreakable bond between the people and the land they call home.

## Table Of Content

Chapter 1: Breakage
Chapter 2: The Prime Clash
Chapter 3: Magical Moss
Chapter 4: One on One
Chapter 5: Rise of a New Dawn
Chapter 6: Spoils of War
Chapter 7: Desperate Measures
Chapter 8: Twisted Quest

King Rono, trapped underground, dreamed of his people's struggle. The British Army had ordered: "Fire the Cannons." Darkness gathered over Juhaka, as the men were ready to fight. Noraa's resolve would soon face its biggest test, and as the battle for survival was about to begin, a glowing figure erupts from the pits into the sky and descends.

# CHAPTER 1

# Breakage

The night air trembled as the British soldiers launched their attack, cannons blazing in the distance. A bomb soared through the air, rolling toward the pits. But before they could reach their target, a brilliant light illuminated the sky as the bomb exploded before reaching its target.

The massive, shiny figure that had emerged from the pit grew brighter, and as it landed, its radiance enveloped Noraa's body. The villagers and soldiers watched in awe as Noraa's form began to shift.

Her limbs lengthened, her muscles bulging beneath her skin. Her face transformed, wrinkles forming onto her features. Her hair turned silver, flowing like a river of moonlight down her back. Armor materialized around her, forged from an otherworldly metal that glistened with a delicate glow.

Noraa now stood as an ancient warrior woman, her eyes blazing with a strong inner light. The transformation sent shivers down the spines of both friend and foe.

The soldiers hesitated, their fingers trembling on the triggers. Fear whispered among them, "What sorcery is this?"

The villagers, inspired by Noraa's metamorphosis, steeled themselves for battle. Sigie, Zuri, and the elders appeared suddenly from behind with determined glances.

As the moon burst forth from the horizon, its half face shining bright, the atmosphere shifted. The air vibrated with an electric energy, instilling both sides with an unspoken knowledge: this night would decide their fate.

Smith, the British commander, regaining his composure, bellowed orders. "Fire at will! Take down that...that thing!"

Cannons roared, and bullets rained toward Noraa. But the warrior woman stood firm, her armour glowing with an inner light. She raised her hands, and the earth responded.

The pits, once passive, now awakened. Volcanic vents of mud and stone erupted, shielding Noraa and the villagers from the barrage. The British soldiers stumbled back, their advance halted in surprise.

As the moon climbed higher, its silvery light danced across the battlefield. Noraa's eyes flashed with a battle-hungry gleam.

"Tonight," she declared, her voice carrying across the chaos, "You fight to stay or run to live!"

THE BRITISH SOLDIERS, undeterred by Noraa's transformation, launched their cannons for the second time. This time, the bombs sailed past Noraa and her people, exploding into the trees behind them. The deafening boom shook the ground, sending splintered wood and leaves flying.

The villagers exchanged worried glances. "The pits' protection is breached," Zuri whispered. Noraa turned to see her grandmother with her brother Sigei. But they gazed at Noraa with surprise as they saw her mysterious form.

Noraa's eyes narrowed. "We must cross the pits to defend."

With newfound determination, the village men readied themselves to face the enemy. Sigie grasped his spear tightly, given to him by Zuri and standing beside Noraa.

The British soldiers, sensing victory within reach, erupted into cheers. "We've broken through!" commander Smith shouted. "Advance, men!"

The soldiers surged forward, daggers glinting in the moonlight. Noraa stood firm, her armour shining.

"Beyond the pits!" she called out. "Defend Juhaka!"

The village men charged forward, Noraa leading the way. As they crossed the pits, the earth trembled beneath their feet. The soldiers closed in, their war cries echoing through the night.

Noraa raised her hands, and the ground responded. Vines and roots burst forth, entwining the soldiers' legs, slowing their advance as they fall down.

"Take cover!" Sigie yelled, as the villagers reached the pits' edge.

They formed a defensive line across, spears and arrows at the ready. Noraa stood at the center, her eyes blazing.

The soldiers, now within range, unleashed a hail of gunfire. Noraa's armour glowed brighter, shielding her from the cascades.

The village men returned fire, their arrows flying true. But the soldiers' numbers seemed endless, and they kept coming as others fell victim to the arrows.

Noraa knew they couldn't hold out for long.

As the half-moon reached its zenith, casting a dim glow over the war-torn landscape, Noraa's radiant armour began to fade. The soldiers, sensing victory within their grasp, intensified their assault. Bullets whizzed past Noraa, kicking up dust and debris.

WITH A MIGHTY CRY, Noraa unleashed a sonic blast that sent the soldiers stumbling backward. The sound wave rippled through the air, knocking men off their feet and silencing the gunfire.

SEIZING THE MOMENT, Noraa swiftly notched two arrows in her bow. Her eyes locked onto the soldiers' commander, now struggling to regain his footing. Her fingers tensed, ready to release the strings.

YET, SHE HESITATED. Waiting for the perfect moment to strike, Noraa held her position, her gaze scanning the chaotic battlefield. The soldiers, regrouping, began to close in once more.

"WAIT FOR THE SIGNAL!" Sigie shouted, his voice carrying above the din. "Let them think we're weakening!"

NORAA NODDED, HER FOCUS unwavering. The moon, now full, cast an otherworldly light upon the scene. The soldiers, unaware of the trap, pressed forward.

THE AIR WAS HEAVY WITH anticipation. Noraa's bow remained firm, her arrows poised for release. The commander, Smith, confident in his advantage, sneered at Noraa.

"TAKE HER DOWN!" HE shouted.

THE SOLDIERS SURGED forward, their guns blazing. Noraa's moment was near.

AS NORAA'S FINGERS prepared to release the bowstrings, faint cries echoed from behind her. The pleas were soft, almost inaudible, but they halted Noraa's motion. Her head wheeled, scanning the darkness beyond the pits.

THE SOLDIERS, OBLIVIOUS to the cries, continued their relentless strikes. Bullets dashed past Noraa, striking the ground and still sending dirt flying. Some villagers, exposed in the open, cried out as they fell, being hit and injured.

"DOWN! EVERYONE, DOWN!" Noraa shouted, quickly refraining from shooting her bow.

THE VILLAGERS HASTILY dropped to the grassy floor, seeking cover. Noraa joined them, flattening herself against the earth. The sudden disappearance of their targets confused the soldiers.

"WHERE DID THEY GO?" a soldier yelled.

"KEEP FIRING!" THE COMMANDER ordered. As he was mounted on his hoarse. "They can't have vanished!"

BUT THE SOLDIERS' SHOTS hit only dirt and grass. Uncertainty crept into their ranks. But Dickson who is an optimist, falls back secretly from the battle.

AS THE GUNFIRE SLOWED, then ceased, an uneasy silence fell over the battlefield. The villagers held their breath, hidden from view. Noraa's ears remained tuned to the faint cries, now slightly louder.

"SIGIE," SHE WHISPERED, "what's happening?"

SIGIE'S VOICE WAS BARELY audible. "I don't know, but it's coming from the pits."

THE CRIES GREW LOUDER, taking on a haunting quality. They seemed to emanate from the very earth itself.

NORAA'S GRIP ON HER bow tightened as she laid down looking forward. Something was stirring, something strange.

## CHAPTER 2

# The Prime Clash

The sudden silence was shattered by the explosive bursting of grass capsules, like nature's own gunfire. The rapid, sharp sounds echoed across the battlefield, captivating both sides.

NORAA, SEIZING THE moment, sprang to her feet, her eyes fixed on the commander at a distance. With fluid motion, she notched the arrow in her bow and released it, sending it soaring skyward.

THE ARROW PIERCED THE air, its trajectory perfect, heading straight for the commander Smith. Time seemed to slow as the soldiers watched, frozen in awe.

AS NORAA'S ARROW SOARED through the air, destined for the commander, a sudden, bony hand materialized out of thin air, mere inches from the commander's face. The hand closed around the arrow, halting its deadly trajectory.

THE COMMANDER'S EYES flickered toward the hand, a hint of a smile playing on his lips.

AN EERIE, GAUNT FIGURE briefly took shape, its presence unsettling. Faded, dark cloaks swelled around it, like smoke coalescing into substance. Then, in an instant, the figure vanished.

THE COMMANDER'S SMILE broadened, his confidence renewed. "You can't harm me," he taunted Noraa.

BEHIND THE SCENES, Zuri, lying prone and guarded, watched the exchange with growing unease. Recognizing the ominous sign, Zuri called out to Noraa in a hushed, urgent tone.

"NORAA, FALL BACK! NOW!

"WHAT PROTECTS HIM... it's not human. We can't take on that kind of power."

NORAA'S GAZE LINGERED on the commander, her mind at work. She knew Zuri's warning wasn't idle. The ghostly figure's brief appearance triggered shivers within her.

Sigie, sensing Noraa's hesitation, whispered, "What do we do, Noraa?"

NORAA'S EYES ON FOCUS. "We retreat, regroup. This isn't a battle we can win tonight."

AS THE GRASS CAPSULES continued bursting, the earth trembled, and an unsettling energy gathered around Commander Smith.

THE COMMANDER, STILL smiling, barked orders to his soldiers. "Fall back! We'll level this place with cannons! Prepare for artillery fire!"

NORAA QUICKLY TURNED to her people. "Retreat! Back to the village, now!"

ZURI'S WARNING STILL echoed in her mind. She knew they couldn't face the commander's mysterious protector.

AS THE VILLAGERS HASTENED toward the pit, Noraa followed, but her feet felt heavy, as if rooted to the ground.

" LET'S MOVE!" SIGIE urged, grabbing her arm.

HOWEVER, NORAA COULDN'T take another step. An unseen force blocked her path, preventing her from crossing the pit.

"WHAT'S WRONG?" SIGIE asked, concern emerged from his face.

NORAA'S EYES WIDENED. "I... I don't know. It's like something's holding me back."

THE VILLAGERS, UNINFORMED to Noraa's struggle, continued their retreat. Zuri, sensing something wrong, rushed back to Noraa's side.

"NORAA, WHAT'S HAPPENING?" Zuri asked, looking around their surroundings.

NORAA STRAINED AGAINST the invisible barrier. "I don't know! It won't let me pass!"

SUDDENLY, THE EARTH beneath them trembled more violently. The bursting grass capsules intensified, and the air thickened with an haunting energy.

SIGIE'S VOICE DROPPED to a whisper. "The pits... they're reacting to you, Noraa."

A FAINT GLOW EMANATED from the pits, illuminating Noraa's stricken face. The villagers, now on the other side, watched in horror as Noraa remained trapped.

As the villagers vanished behind the safety of their homes, Noraa remained alone, trapped by the mysterious force. The pits' glow intensified, enveloping her.

SUDDENLY, THE EARTH shook violently, and a towering wall erupted from the ground, encircling the village. The barrier was thicker and higher than never before, fortified with ancient, weathered stones and mud.

CANNONS BOOMED IN THE distance, their thunderous roar shaking the ground. Bombs began to rain on, exploding against the new wall with booming crashes.

INSIDE THE VILLAGE, panic spread. "Where's Noraa?" someone cried.

ZURI'S FACE TWISTED with worry. "She was right behind us!"

SIGIE SPRANG INTO ACTION, taking command. "Everyone, get to your homes! Now!"

# 16

AS THE VILLAGERS SCATTERED, Sigie turned to Zuri. "We need to rescue Noraa!

"BUT FIRST, MAKE SURE everyone's safe. I'll check the walls."

ZURI OLD BUT ENERGETIC woman, nodded, dashing off to coordinate the villagers.

SIGIE SPRINTED ALONG the wall, assessing its strength. Bombs pounded the barrier, but it held firm.

OUTSIDE, NORAA STOOD frozen, the pits' glow still surrounding her. The wall's construction seemed to have drained her energy.

AS THE BOMBARDMENT intensified, Noraa's vision blurred. She stumbled, falling to one knee.

SIGIE SPRINTED TOWARD the breached wall, determined to reach Noraa. But as he began to climb, the wall suddenly and unexpectedly extended upwards, towering above him.

THE STONES SEEMED TO grow, lengthening and thickening, forming an impassable barrier. Sigie's hands slipped, and he fell back, his ascent foiled.

"NO!" SIGIE SHOUTED, frustration and concern appearing on his face.

UNSHAKEABLE, SIGIE tried again, but the wall continued to rise, its height lengthened. The extension was relentless, blocking Sigie's path.

"IT'S IMPOSSIBLE," SIGIE muttered, discouraged. "Noraa..."

WITH A HEAVY HEART, Sigie retreated, forced to abandon his attempt to reach Noraa as the striking sounds of the bombs convinced him.

AS HE REJOINED THE villagers, Zuri approached him. "Sigie, what happened?"

SIGIE'S EYES REFLECTED his worry. "The wall... it won't let me pass. Noraa's alone."

## 18

ZURI'S EXPRESSION TURNED harsh . "We need to find another way."

MEANWHILE, NORAA STOOD alone, to face whatever was around her.

# CHAPTER 3

# Magical Moss

As Sigie, Zuri, and the village men retreated to the safety of their homes, the soldiers continued their unstoppable fire. Noraa, isolated by the mysterious wall, strengthened herself for the impending confrontation.

THE MOONLIGHT WANED, casting a creepy darkness over the landscape. The bursting grass capsules ceased, resulting in silence.

SUDDENLY, THE WALLS at the pits, now quiet and still, began to yield their secrets. Majestic statues, previously hidden, emerged from the depths. Each figure took on human form, standing beside Noraa.

ENCASED IN ANCIENT warrior attire, these newfound allies exuded an atmosphere of strength and loyalty. Sophisticated, moss-like patterns adorned their armour, glowing softly in the diminishing light.

THE VILLAGERS, WATCHING from a distance, marveled at a miraculous sight as the sky turned a greenish glint within their sight Juhaka.

"BY THE ANCESTORS," Zuri whispered. "The Guardians of the Pits."
 "What do you mean?" Sigie asked.

MEANWHILE, THE COMMANDER'S smile faltered as Xarath materialized before him. Two dark, creatures, resembling black ghosts with piercing red eyes, flanked Xarath.

"THESE ARE ON MY SIDE," Xarath declared, his voice dripping with cruelty. "They will ensure your victory."

THE COMMANDER'S CONFIDENCE renewed, he ordered the soldiers to rearrange for another assault.

AS THE CANNONS RELOADED, Noraa stood tall, surrounded by her newfound allies. The magical moss on their armour pulsed with energy, synchronizing their heartbeats.

THE LEAD GUARDIAN, an imposing figure with moss-covered shoulders but in a human frame, addressed Noraa. "We have awaited this moment. Our bond with the land will not be broken. I am Rono, King of Juhaka "

WITH A SMILING NOD, Noraa drew her bow, its string vibrating with anticipation.

XARATH SNEERED, HIS airy form rippling with dark energy. "You think these relics can stand against the Shadowborn?"

THE GUARDIANS FORMED a cohort around Noraa, ready to face the impending battle.

AS THE MOON DIPPED below the horizon, the stage was set for an epic clash:

NORAA AND THE GUARDIANS of the Pits vs. the Commander, Xarath, and the Shadowborn.

Sigie's curiosity got the better of him. "Zuri, what are these Guardians of the Pits?"

ZURI'S EYES REMAINED fixed on the distant battle occurrence. "They're ancient warriors, sworn to protect our land."

SIGIE'S GAZE FOLLOWED Zuri's. "And Rono? Who is he?"

ZURI'S VOICE TOOK ON a reverent tone. "Rono, the King of Juhaka, has risen from the pits. We saw the greenish glint in the sky – a sign of his return."

THE VILLAGERS EXCHANGED awestruck whispers and Sigie remembered when Zuri once mentioned him sometime ago.

"BUT THERE'S MORE," Zuri cautioned. "Our greatest enemy, Xarath, has also emerged."

SIGIE'S BROW FURROWED. "Xarath? Who is he?"

ZURI'S EXPRESSION TURNED grim. "A dark wizard, expelled from our village for his evil ways many years ago. He seeks to destroy everything we hold dear."

GASPS SPREAD THROUGH the gathering.

"ONE OF OUR OWN?" A villager whispered.

ZURI NODDED. "XARATH'S thirst for power consumed him. Rono and the Guardians protected us then; they'll do so again."

THE VILLAGERS' FACES set with determination.

SIGIE'S VOICE WAS RESOLUTE. "We stand with Noraa, Rono, and the Guardians."

ZURI'S EXPRESSION TURNED serious. "Let's move back to the village, for your safety. I'll explain everything."

THE VILLAGERS NODDED, following Zuri and Sigie away from the pits to the huts.

AS THEY WALKED, ANTICIPATION hung in the air. Would Noraa and the Guardians emerge victorious?

BUT UPON REACHING THE village center, Zuri began to clarify the mysteries.

"THE GUARDIANS OF THE Pit," Zuri started, "are not just mere statues. They were once hunters and ordinary people, trapped outside the pit when they failed to return before sunset by turning into mud statues and vanishing before the next morning as you know already."

"TRAPPED?" SIGIE REPEATED. "What happens to them?"

ZURI'S VOICE TOOK ON a solemn tone. "They become the Guardians, sworn to protect Juhaka and its people."

A VILLAGER WHISPERED, "But what about Xarath?"

ZURI'S EYES CLOUDED. "Xarath is not alone. He commands the Shadowborn, elite warriors infused with dark energy."

MURMURS OF FEAR RIPPLED through the crowd as they held sticks in their hands burning with fire.

"SHADOWBORN?" A VILLAGER repeated, trembling.

ZURI NODDED GRAVELY. "They were once humans of our land, but Xarath's dark magic twisted them. Now, they serve only him."

SIGIE'S FACE PALED. "How many Shadowborn are there?"

ZURI HESITATED BEFORE answering, "Two, each with unique abilities and strengths."

THE VILLAGERS EXCHANGED frightened glances.

A VILLAGER INTEROGATED, "What chance does Noraa have against such foes?"

ZURI'S EXPRESSION TURNED resolute. "Rono and the Guardians will aid her. Together, they can defeat Xarath and the Shadowborn."

"But why did you conceal all this until now?" Sigie asked.

Zuri kept mute and dashed towards the elders residence as they followed.

But doubt lingered, casting a shadow over the village.

## CHAPTER 4

# One on One

Noraa, King Rono, and the Guardians of the Pit stood ready, facing Xarath, Kandi, Suuj _ the Shadowborn, and commander Smith's army.

THE BRITISH ARMY, ONCE steadfast behind the commander, faltered, abandoning their posts. Fear claimed the soldiers as they fled, leaving their leader to fate.

XARATH DISDAINED, HIS eyes lashing with energy. "You think you can end this?"

Rono drew his sword, its blade shining with ancient power. "We will protect this land, no matter the cost."

NORAA NOCKED AN ARROW in her bow, its string trilling with magic. "Let's end this."

KANDI, THE UNYIELDING shadowborn, standing strong, his massive frame radiating volcanic energy. Suuj, the Phantom shadowborn, hovered beside him, her ethereal form weaving illusions.

THE COMMANDER WATCHED, fascinated, as the battle unfolded.

CLASHING STEEL AND exploding magic shook the battlefield. Noraa's arrows flew true, striking Kandi with precision. Rono's sword sliced through Suuj's deceptions.

XARATH HURLED DARK energy blasts, shattering the earth. The other Guardians of the Pit stood firm, their bond and magic amplifying.

KANDI'S HAMMER BLOWS crushed the ground, sending Noraa stumbling. Suuj's illusions enveloped Rono, obscuring his vision.

THE COMMANDER'S EYES widened as Noraa and Rono fought on, undaunted.

THE BATTLE RAGED, ANCIENT magic clashing with dark energy:

NORAA'S ARROWS IGNITED with great force;
    Rono's sword shone brighter, cleaving shadows;
    Kandi hammer shattered stone, sending boulders crashing;
    Suuj's deceptions danced, deceiving the eye.

AS THE FIGHT INTENSIFIED, the landscape trembled:

TREES SPLINTERED;ROCKS shattered;The earth cracked.

THE COMMANDER'S FASCINATION turned to horror. "This is madness!"

XARATH'S LAUGHTER ECHOED through the chaos. "This is power!"

NORAA AND RONO FOUGHT on, determined to protect their land.

BUT THE BATTLE RAGED on, Noraa facing Kandi and Suuj's, while Rono clashed with Xarath.

NORAA'S AGILITY PROVED unmatched as she dodged Kandi's crushing blows. Her arrows flew swift and true, striking the Shadowborn's weak points.

SUUJ'S ILLUSIONS ENGULFED Noraa, but she countered with her own magic, dispelling the deception. Noraa's bow sang with a strong melody, unleashing:

Piercing Kandi's darkness; Dispersing Suuj's illusions and scorching the Shadowborn's essence.

KANDI STUMBLED, HIS massive frame wavering. Suuj's ethereal form began to unravel.

MEANWHILE, RONO FACED Xarath, their clash shaking the earth:

RONO'S SWORD SLICED through Xarath's dark energy blasts;
    Xarath's spells cracked the ground, but Rono stood firm.

THE COMMANDER WATCHED, as Rono unleashed by shattering Xarath's defenses; Deflecting dark energy and unleashing swift, relentless blows.

XARATH STUMBLED, HIS powers waning.

"IMPOSSIBLE!" XARATH shouted. "You're no match for me!"

RONO STOOD TALL, HIS sword shining brighter. "I am the King of Juhaka. My people's legacy will not be defeated."

THE COMMANDER'S EYES widened as Rono's strength and determination became clear.

NORAA TOOK ADVANTAGE of Kandi's weakness, striking the final blow by piercing Kandi's heart.

SUUJ'S FANTASIES DISSIPATED, her essence vanishing.

KANDI COLLAPSED, DEFEATED.

XARATH'S EYES BLAZED with fury.

"YOU MAY HAVE BESTED my Shadowborn," Xarath snarled, "but I will crush you!"

RONO STOOD READY.

THE SHADOWBORN DEFEATED, the British commander fled, abandoning Xarath. His soldiers had already deserted, fleeing to their makeshift base deep in the woods.

XARATH STOOD ALONE, facing Rono and Noraa. The Guardians of the Pit stood watched and vigilant.

SUDDENLY, XARATH PRODUCED a mysterious horn from his cloak. Its surface is etched with evil runes.

XARATH BLEW THE HORN, its sound echoing through the land. The villagers, distant but listening, felt a shiver run down their spines.

THE HORN'S CALL AWAKENED dark serpents, colossal bodies emerging from the earth behind Xarath. They slithered toward Noraa, Rono, and the Guardians.

BUT THE GUARDIANS OF the Pit didn't falter. United, they leaped into the sky, landing before Rono and Noraa. Their eyes blazed with ancient power.

"PROTECT THEM!" ONE'S voice echoed.

GUARDIANS CLASHED WITH serpents;
   Rono and Noraa retreated, overwhelmed;
   The earth shook; the sky darkened.

THE GUARDIANS FOUGHT effortlessly:
   Rono and Noraa watched, awestruck: "This is unbelievable!" Noraa exclaimed.
   "We must help!" Noraa urged.

BUT THE GUARDIANS HELD firm:

"FALL BACK!" ONE OF them ordered. "We'll hold the line!"

THE SERPENTS' RELENTLESS assault pushed Rono and Noraa further back.

AS SUDDENLY AS THEY appeared, the dark serpents dissipated, their defeated bodies crumbling to dust.

XARATH VANISHED, LEAVING behind an creepy silence.

THE BATTLE PAUSED, Noraa turned to Rono. "Let's return to the village. The people will need reassurance."

RONO NODDED, MASKING his sword. "Agreed. We've earned a brief respite."

TOGETHER, THEY TURNED to leave.

BEHIND THEM, THE GUARDIANS of the Pit stood vigilant, their mission accomplished.

A SOFT BREEZE WHISPERED through, carrying the essence of the Magical Moss away from their bodies.

THE GUARDIANS' BODIES began to disintegrate.
 Their dissolution resembled the gentle dispersal of leaves on an autumn breeze.

ONE AMONG THEM, WHISPERED, "Our duty fulfilled...may Juhaka heal."

NORAA AND RONO TURNED back, witnessing the Guardians' disappearance.

"MAY THEIR SACRIFICE not be forgotten," Rono said, reverence in his voice.

NORAA BOWED HER HEAD. "Their memory will live on.
 A sense of loss mingled with relief.

AS THE DUST SETTLED, Noraa and Rono walked toward the village in the middle of the night.
 The commander's fleeing army, Xarath's unknown plans, and the mysterious horn's significance lingered, unsettling.

BUT FOR NOW, THE VILLAGE was safe.

# CHAPTER 5

# Rise of a New Dawn

Rono and Noraa walked into the village, greeted by jubilant villagers in the dark. Their transformation shocked the crowd:

Noraa had transformed back to her normal self and stood as a youthful, radiant woman;

Rono, the mighty King, had transformed into an older man, worn by time.

DESPITE THIS, THE VILLAGERS rejoiced: drums pounded out victorious rhythms; songs of praise filled the air; cheers and shouts hailed Rono and Noraa.

THE VILLAGERS SWARMED, thanking their heroes:
"Long live King Rono!"
"Blessings upon Noraa, our savior!"
"May their names be remembered in history!"

RONO SMILED, HIS AGED eyes twinkling. "Our land is reborn. Let us rebuild." Noraa's youthful face glowed. "We'll create a brighter future."

THE FESTIVITIES CONTINUED: feasting; dancing; praises.

AS NIGHT FELL DEEPER, one of the village elders, Akara, approached Rono and Noraa. "Your transformation is a mystery," Akara said, "but your bravery remains unchanged."

Rono chuckled. "Age is but a number. Our hearts remain strong." Noraa nodded. "We'll continue to protect our home."

The villagers cheered, their admiration for Rono and Noraa growing. But amidst the celebration, whispers spread:

"What caused their transformation?" "Are we free now?"

THE DAWN BREAKS, USHERING in a new era.

FOUR DAYS PASSED, AND the village remained peaceful. Zuri, Noraa's wise grandmother, sought out Noraa. "Noraa, I must share with you," Zuri said, her eyes twinkling. "King Rono, the hero who saved our land, has no heir."

NORAA'S CURIOSITY ENTICED. "What do you mean?" Zuri's smile hinted at mischief. "Rono never married, nor had children."

NORAA'S EYES WIDENED. "Why are you telling me this, Grandma?" Zuri's hands clasped Noraa's. "I want you to consider marrying King Rono."

NORAA RECOILED. "NO! He's...old. I cannot." Zuri chuckled. "Age is but a number. Rono's heart remains strong."

NORAA HESITATED, UNSURE. Zuri persisted. "Think of the unity it would bring. You'd secure our village's future."

Weeks passed, Zuri's words dancing in Noraa's mind.

Sigie happens to confront Noraa constructively to aid Zuri in convincing Noraa to marry King Rono. But Noraa was not close to igniting any affection for Rono.

But Zuri knew what a bond between Noraa and Rono could yield. Zuri happens to be one of the old women of Juhaka who qualifies to be called as an elder of the Kings. She knew the secrets of Juhaka as well as the eldest of the elders, Akara. They knew all about Juhaka.

Compromisations ensued:

Rono, though older, showed unwavering dedication; Noraa, despite reservations, saw Rono's kindness.

The village elder, Akara, officiated the union. Noraa and Rono exchanged vows beneath the shades of the large oak tree at the palace.

THE VILLAGERS REJOICED: drums beat; singers performed; dancers spun.

RONO SMILED, HIS EYES shining. "You're my queen, Noraa." Noraa's heart swelled. "I'll stand by you, King Rono."

Zuri and Sigie smiled in awe as they sighted the bright couple.

Their love blossomed, bridging the age gap. As night fell, the village celebrated.

The newlyweds' happiness was palpable.

THE PASSAGE OF TIME had brought about a profound transformation in the village. Once plagued by fear and uncertainty, the village had blossomed into a haven of peace and harmony.

At the heart of this change lay the unwavering dedication of its leaders, particularly Sigie, the newly appointed Chief in Command of the warriors of Juhaka as he was now a young man.

Under his guidance, the village's borders remained secure, harmony flourished, and innovation thrived.

THE VILLAGERS, ONCE bound by fear, now rejoiced in their newfound freedom. Children played without inhibition, their laughter spreading through the paths in the village.

Elders shared their wisdom, imparting valuable lessons to the younger generation.

Hunters ventured forth with confidence, returning with bounty to nourish their families. The village's revival was a testament to the power of effective leadership and collective endurance.

AT THE FOREFRONT OF this endurance stood Rono and Noraa, the village's beloved leaders. Their marriage, once a symbol of hope, had thrived into a beacon of inspiration.

Together, they nurtured the village, imparting wisdom and kindness. Their love had grown stronger, radiating warmth and comfort to all who surrounded them.

As they walked among their people, hands entwined, their presence seemed to embody the very essence of harmony.

ONE SUNNY DAY, SIGIE led his team on a successful hunting expedition, further solidifying the village's prosperity. The forest yielded its bounty, providing an abundance of game.

The village celebrated, feasting on meats, singing joyful melodies, and dancing under cosmic skies. Rono and Noraa joined, their faces aglow with happiness. "Sigie, your leadership brings joy and prosperity," Rono praised, his eyes shining with gratitude. Noraa nodded in agreement, "Our village prospers under your careful guidance."

AS NIGHT FELL, THE village slept peacefully, pacified by the soothing sounds of crickets, gentle breezes, and moonlit skies.

Amidst this tranquility, whispers of a prophecy began to circulate. "A new generation rises, with Rono's wisdom and Noraa's heart, a brighter future unfolds, where love, peace, and harmony entwine."

The wind carried these whispers, seeding hope and promise. Villagers wondered about the prophecy's meaning, speculating about the future leaders who would carry forth Rono and Noraa's legacy.

THE VILLAGE'S FUTURE seemed bright, filled with possibility, growth, and unity. As the villagers looked to the horizon, they knew that their collective efforts would continue to shape their destiny.

Sigie's bravery, Rono and Noraa's guidance, and the village's resilience would ensure a prosperous tomorrow.

The rise of a new dawn had brought about a transformation, one that would endure for generations to come.

AS THE VILLAGE CONTINUED to thrive, the prophecy's words resonated, a reminder of the limitless potential that lay ahead. The villagers remained steadfast, united in their pursuit of peace, harmony, and prosperity.

And as they walked into the future, they carried with them the wisdom of their leaders, the love of their community, and the unwavering hope for a brighter tomorrow.

# CHAPTER 6

# Spoils of war

The aftermath of the battle had left an indelible mark on the commander's army. As he stood amidst the makeshift base, he was met with the grim reality of death and desertion.

The once-mighty force was now dwindled, with soldiers laid to rest and captains and sergeants counting their losses. The air was heavy with sorrow, and commander Smith knew he had to act quickly to rekindle the flames of ambition within his men.

WITH A STEADFAST GAZE, the commander addressed his troops. "We cannot leave now. Our mission remains incomplete," he declared, his voice persistent. However, his words were met with resistance.

The soldiers, drained from battle and burdened by loss, murmured among themselves. "We've lost many. It's time to return to Europe," they whispered. The commander sensed the desperation in their voices and knew he had to tread carefully.

HE BEGAN TO PACE, HIS words dripping with persuasion. "Think of the riches, the slaves, the glory awaiting us. Juhaka's people will fetch a handsome price," he promised, painting a vivid picture of the spoils of war. Some soldiers hesitated, tempted by the promise of wealth and fame.

Others stood firm, their resolve unshaken. "We vowed to leave. Our families await," they countered, their voices firm.

THE COMMANDER'S EXPRESSION darkened, his eyes narrowing. "Very well," he conceded. "You may request leave, but for now, you will stay." The soldiers nodded, submissive but unreconciled.

Their planned departure loomed, a deadline set. For now, they would bide their time, awaiting the day they could escape the commander's grasp.

AS THE SOLDIERS DISPERSED, whispers spread like wildfire. "Will we truly leave?", "What horrors await Juhaka?"

The commander, unaware to the non-conformity, smiled to himself. His obsession with Juhaka's capture burned brighter, fueled by the setbacks. He began to plot, weaving a web of strategy and deception.

THE SOLDIERS' RELUCTANCE would soon be tested, their loyalty pushed to the breaking point. The commander's resolve remained unwavering, his focus fixed on the prize.

Juhaka's people, still basking in the glow of their hard-won peace, were unaware of the gathering storm. The commander's plans would soon unfold, threatening to upend the fragile harmony.

AS THE DAYS PASSED, tensions warmed, awaiting the spark that would ignite the flames of conflict. The commander's army, torn between duty and desire, stood at a crossroads.

Would they follow their leader into the abyss, or would they find the courage to defy him?

IN THE REALMS, A MALICIOUS figure veiled, awaiting the perfect moment to strike. Xarath, fueled by vengeance and ambition, had been tracking the commander. One fateful night, he found his opportunity.

WITH FAST AND DEADLY precision, Xarath ended the commander's life. As the commander's body collapsed, Xarath began to transform, assuming his form.

THE DARK SORCERY OF shape-shifting allowed Xarath to perfectly replicate the commander's appearance, voice, and mannerisms. The impersonation was flawless. He got rid of the commander's body in a vanish.

DAYS PASSED, AND THE soldiers noticed a change in their leader's demeanor. His resolve seemed renewed, his determination firm. Unbeknownst to them, Xarath now pulled the strings.

"THE PITS ARE BROKEN, Juhaka's defenses weakened," Xarath declared, rallying his troops. "Our final invasion approaches." Seduced by promises of wealth, luxury, and hidden gunpowder, the soldiers' hesitation dissipated, replaced by excitement.

"WE'LL FOLLOW YOU, COMMANDER Smith!" they chorused, oblivious to Xarath's true identity. The dark sorcerer enjoyed in his deception, orchestrating their descent into chaos.

WEEKS PASSED, AS THE army prepared for the impending assault. Drills intensified, strategies unfolded, and morale soared. Xarath's plan was unfolding with precision, fueled by his thirst for power and revenge.

JUHAKA'S PEOPLE REMAINED blissfully unaware of the gathering storm, their peaceful existence on the cusp of destruction. Xarath's evil presence now drove the army's actions, ensuring a disastrous confrontation.

AS TENSIONS MOUNTED, the fate of Juhaka hung in the balance. Would anyone uncover Xarath's deception, or would his dark magic seal the village's doom?

BUT QUIET SO, AMONG the ranks of devoted soldiers, a lone individual sensed an unsettling anomaly. Dickson, a battle-hardened soldier, detected a subtle inconsistency in his commander's behaviour. Initially, it was a fleeting glance, a hint of unfamiliarity that Dickson attributed to fatigue. However, as the days passed, the feeling persisted.

THE COMMANDER'S MANNERISMS, once familiar and reassuring, now seemed forced and artificial.

His voice, though identical in tone and pitch, carried an unsettling undertone that only Dickson seemed to notice. His instincts screamed warning, prompting him to reevaluate his leader's behavior.

DESPITE HIS GROWING unease, Dickson kept his suspicions hidden, locked away in his mind. He continued to follow orders, falling in line with his comrades and maintaining a steadfast exterior.

Outwardly, he remained loyal; inwardly, he began to weave a plan to uncover the truth.

DICKSON'S THOUGHTS swirled with questions. "What has changed? Is this truly our commander?" He searched for cracks in the facade, any hint of deception that might explain his reservations.

As the army marched toward Juhaka, Dickson's resolve hardened. He would uncover the truth, no matter the cost.

UNNOTICED TO XARATH, the dark sorcerer who had assumed the commander's form, a silent adversary had emerged.

Dickson's quiet determination would soon challenge Xarath's grip on the army. Dickson's investigation would delve into the heart of the deception, potentially upending the entire campaign.

AS THE TENSION MOUNTED, Dickson walked a precarious tightrope. His loyalty to the army and his duty to uncover the truth hung in the balance. Would he succeed in exposing Xarath, or would the dark sorcerer's powers prove too great to overcome?

# CHAPTER 7

# Desperate Measures

The village of Juhaka had witnessed the blissful union of King Rono and Noraa, a love that had brought hope and joy to its residents. However, fate had other plans, and the village was soon engulfed in sorrow.

Zuri, a pillar of the community, succumbed to a sudden and devastating illness. Her condition rapidly deteriorated, leaving the villagers shocked and helpless. Despite the best efforts of Juhaka's healers, Zuri's life slipped away, leaving behind a trail of grief and despair.

NORAA, PARTICULARLY, was consumed by anguish. Her mentor, confidante, and beloved friend had vanished, leaving an unfillable void. Sigie, sensing Noraa's distress, rallied around her, offering a shoulder to cry on and a comforting presence. But before the village could even begin to heal from Zuri's passing, disaster struck again.

RONO, NORAA'S BELOVED husband, fell prey to a mysterious affliction. His health began to decline at an alarming rate, defying the understanding of Juhaka's medical experts.

Desperate measures were taken to save Rono, but fate seemed determined to snatch him away. The villagers watched in horror as Rono's vitality got away, his once-strong spirit crushed by an unseen force.

RONO'S PASSING SENT shockwaves through Juhaka, igniting fears and suspicions. Dark magic and ancient curses were whispered about in hushed tones. The village, once a sanctuary, now seemed vulnerable to malevolent forces. Noraa's world lay shattered, her heart heavy with grief. Sigie struggled to console her, but his efforts seemed futile against the crushing weight of her sorrow.

AS JUHAKA MOURNED, an unsettling silence descended upon the village. It was clear that an evil presence lurked, threatening the very fabric of their existence.

What evil force had claimed Zuri and Rono? Was it mere coincidence or a calculated assault? The villagers' fears demanded answers, but the truth remained unrevealed.

AKARA, THE WISE AND revered village elder, gathered the residents of Juhaka. With a gentle yet firm tone, he urged calm and composure. "My dear friends, we must not let fear and uncertainty consume us. We have lost two beloved members, but we must find strength in our unity."

AKARA PROPOSED A SOLEMN ritual to honor Zuri and Rono's memories. "Let us offer sacrifices to our ancestors, seeking guidance and protection in these sad times." The villagers nodded in agreement, finding solace in the familiar traditions.

HOWEVER, A SURPRISE announcement followed. "As is our custom, the time has come to crown a new leader. Noraa, as Rono's partner, is the rightful heir to the throne since she has no son yet." The villagers expected Noraa to accept the crown, but she shocked them with her refusal.

OVERWHELMED BY GRIEF, Noraa's emotional conflict rendered her unable to bear the weight of leadership. "I cannot," she pleaded, her voice trembling. "My heart is shattered. I fear I would fail our village."

AFTER A MOMENT'S CONTEMPLATION, Noraa proposed an alternative. "Sigie, now a young man, has grown wise beyond his years. His compassion, courage, and wisdom make him an ideal leader. Let him be our king, and I shall support him when the need arises."

THE VILLAGERS WERE taken aback but recognized the sense in Noraa's words. Sigie's transformation from a curious youth to a capable young adult had been remarkable. His empathy and kindness had earned their respect.

WITH NORAA'S BLESSING, the villagers fell rightly to her request. Akara, sensing the will of the people, proclaimed Sigie the new king. The young man's surprise gave way to determination as he accepted the task.

AS SIGIE ADORNED THE crown, a mix of emotions swirled within him. He vowed to honor Zuri and Rono's memories, protect his people, and guide Juhaka through the treacherous times ahead.

NORAA, RELIEVED OF the burden, retreated to her but in the palace. Though her heart remained heavy, she found solace in knowing that Sigie would lead their village with wisdom and compassion.

AS NIGHT FELL, THE village began to heal, their collective grief slowly giving way to hope. Yet, in the shadows, whispers persisted – whispers of dark forces, ancient curses, and the true nature of Zuri and Rono's untimely demise.

DAYS HAD PASSED SINCE Sigie's coronation, and Juhaka had begun to heal. A sense of normalcy returned, but Noraa harbored a secret.

She had been experiencing unusual symptoms – fatigue, nausea, and an unshakeable feeling of transformation within. At first, she dismissed the signs, attributing them to grief. But as the days went by, the reality became undeniable: Noraa was pregnant.

THE NEWS SHOULD HAVE brought joy, but instead, it filled her with anguish. How could she carry a child when Rono, her beloved husband, was no longer by her side? The thought of raising a child alone, without the father's love and guidance, overwhelmed her.

Shame crept in, as if she had betrayed Rono's memory. Noraa struggled to reconcile her emotions, torn between the life growing within her and the sorrow that still consumed her.

SHE COULDN'T BEAR THE thought of facing the villagers, fearing their judgment and pity. Nora's initial plan was to confide in Sigie, but her fear of his concern and compassion kept her silent.

The weight of her secret became crushing, and Noraa knew she had to escape. One fateful night, under the light of a full moon, she made up her mind to leave Juhaka, abandoning the only home she had ever known.

WITHOUT A WORD TO ANYONE, Nora packed a small bag and slipped out of the village, disappearing into the darkness. She aimed to seek a new life, free from the painful reminders of her past.

As she vanished into the unknown, Noraa left behind a village that had loved and supported her.

THE NEXT MORNING DAWNED, casting a warm glow over Juhaka. The villagers stirred, beginning their daily routines. Sigie, however, was already abreast with urgency. He dispatched a messenger to Noraa's hut, summoning her to the palace for an important discussion.

BUT WHEN THE MESSENGER arrived, Noraa was nowhere to be found. Her quarters were empty, her belongings seemed untouched. A sense of unease crept over the messenger's face as he hastened back to the Sigie.

SIGIE'S EXPRESSION darkened upon hearing the news. "Find Noraa!" he commanded, his voice echoing through the palace corridors. "Search every corner of Juhaka, every home, everywhere. Leave no stone unturned."

THE PALACE GUARDS SPRANG into action, fanning out across the village. They knocked on doors, inquired with villagers, and scoured the paths.

As the sun climbed higher, Sigie's anxiety grew. He ordered the search party to expand their scope, venturing beyond Juhaka's borders. Horsemen galloped off towards neighboring villages, while foot guards combed the surrounding forests.

"FIND HER!" SIGIE URGED, his voice carrying across the landscape. "Bring her back to us, safe and sound." His eyes scanned around, willing Noraa to appear.

BUT AS THE DAY WORE on, hope began to lose its way. The search party returned, exhausted and empty-handed. Sigie's face fell, his heart heavy with concern.

"WE WILL NOT REST UNTIL Noraa is found," he vowed, his voice resolute. "Prepare a team to scout farther lands. Leave no village unvisited, no bush unsearched."

AS NIGHT DESCENDED, Juhaka's residents gathered, their faces aglow with burning branches and lanterns. Prayers and whispers filled the air, all seeking Nora's safe return.

# CHAPTER 8

# Twisted Quest

Xarath, a cunning and ruthless commander, stood before his army, his voice dripping with deception. "Men, today we embark on a glorious mission!

We will capture the natives of Juhaka, reclaiming them for the European markets. We will seize their gunpowder, riches, and women. The spoils of war will be ours!"

THE SOLDIERS CHEERED, fueled by promises of wealth and power. But Xarath's true intentions remained hidden, even from his most trusted lieutenants. Deep within, he burned with an boundless ambition – to rule Juhaka, to claim its throne, and to reign supreme.

UNAWARE TO XARATH, the landscape of Juhaka had shifted. Noraa, the rightful queen, had vanished, and Sigie, a young and determined leader, now wore the crown. The dynamics of power had changed, setting the stage for a clash of what seemed the biggest.

AS XARATH'S ARMY MARCHED towards Juhaka, their commander's mind replayed his strategy. He would crush the villagers' spirits, exploit their resources, and enslave their people. The thought of dominating Juhaka's fertile lands and strategic trade routes sent shivers down his spine.

BUT XARATH WAS OBLIVIOUS to the violent shift in Juhaka's leadership. He envisioned Noraa and Rono, the vulnerable characters, cowering before him. Little did he know that Sigie, the new king, stood ready to defend his people, his land, and his legacy.

THE SUN BEGAN ITS DESCENT, casting long shadows across the landscape. Xarath's army heading to Juhaka's borders, their battle cry resonating through the valley. The villagers, still reeling from Noraa's disappearance, were about to face a new and formidable foe.

XARATH'S ARMY, A FORMIDABLE force driven by ambition and greed, closed in on the village borders. Uninformed to Sigie, the village's hunters had ventured far afield, seeking game for the evening's meal. Their chance encounter with the approaching army sparked a frantic rush to alert their leader.

WITH HASTE, THE HUNTERS sprinted back to Juhaka, their footsteps pounding out a desperate rhythm. Breathless, they burst into Sigie's chambers, their urgent cries echoing through the halls.

"YOUR MAJESTY!" THEY exclaimed. "The British army approaches! We must act swiftly, or risk everything!"

SIGIE'S FACE SET IN determination, his eyes burning with resolve. "Sound the war drums!" he commanded, his voice echoing across the landscape. "We will defend our land, our people, and our legacy!"

AS THE DRUMS BOOMED, Juhaka's villagers rallied, their faces etched with concern. Sigie, resolute, led the charge, his warriors forming battle lines. "We will not yield!" he declared, his voice carrying across the landscape. "We will fight for our freedom, our families, and our future!"

MEANWHILE, NORAA STUMBLED through the wilderness, lost and alone. Hunger and thirst gnawed at her, her unborn child weighing heavy in her womb.

The isolation had taken its toll, her ancestral powers eerily silent. As night descended, Noraa collapsed beneath a twisted tree, exhaustion claiming her.

SUDDENLY, A FLOCK OF glowing white birds materialized above her. Their ethereal song enveloped her, drawing her into a mystical realm. Noraa's eyes widened, her mind disoriented. The birds descended, their gentle touch igniting a surge of energy within her.

AS THE WORLD AROUND her blurred, Noraa felt an ancient connection stirring. The land itself seemed to awaken, energies coursing through the earth. The white birds' presence hinted at a deeper purpose, a hidden destiny waiting to unfold.

BACK AT JUHAKA'S BORDERS, Xarath's army formed battle lines. Sigie's warriors stood ready, their hearts ablaze with determination.

But among the chaos, Dickson still harbored doubts. Was their commander truly who he claimed to be? Or was he an imposter, manipulating them for cruel purposes?

THE SOLDIER'S GAZE narrowed, his finger tightening around his rifle. The fate of Juhaka hung in the balance. Would Sigie's warriors prevail, or would Xarath's army crush their spirits? And what secrets lay hidden within Noraa's twisted quest?

Milton Keynes UK
Ingram Content Group UK Ltd.
UKHW020758231024
450026UK00001B/103